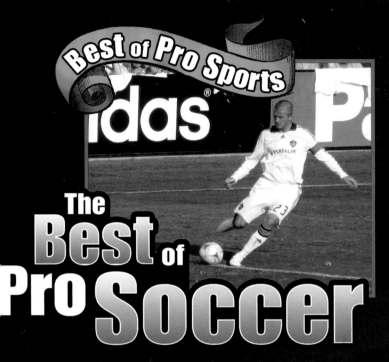

The Best of Pro Soccer

by Heather Adamson

Consultant:
Craig R. Coenen, PhD
Associate Professor of History
Mercer County Community College
West Windsor, New Jersey

Capstone
press

Mankato, Minnesota

First Facts is published by Capstone Press,
151 Good Counsel Drive, P.O. Box 669, Mankato, Minnesota 56002.
www.capstonepub.com

072010
005866R

 Books published by Capstone Press are manufactured with paper
containing at least 10 percent post-consumer waste.

Library of Congress Cataloging-in-Publication Data
Adamson, Heather, 1974–
    The best of pro soccer / by Heather Adamson.
      p. cm. — (First facts. Best of pro sports)
    Includes bibliographical references and index.
    Summary: "Presents some of the best moments and players in professional soccer
history" — Provided by publisher.
      ISBN 978-1-4296-3331-4 (library binding)
      ISBN 978-1-4296-3878-4 (softcover)
      1. Soccer — History — Juvenile literature. 2. Soccer players — Biography — Juvenile
literature. I. Title. II. Series.
GV943.25.A32 2010
796.334'6409 — dc22   2009001178

Editorial Credits
Christopher Harbo, editor; Kyle Grenz, designer; Eric Gohl, media researcher

Photo Credits
AP Images/Kevork Djansezian, 19 (left); Manu Fernandez, 10
BigStockPhoto.com/Ken Durden, 1
Comstock Images, soccer ball
Getty Images Inc./AFP, 13; AFP/Filippo Monteforte, cover; AFP/Greg Wood, 14; AFP/
    Timothy A. Clary, 9 (left); Bob Thomas, 9 (right); Bongarts/Andreas Rentz, 21 (right);
    Central Press, 21 (left); Popperfoto, 4; Popperfoto/Rolls Press, 7; Time & Life
    Pictures/Art Rickerby, 17
Newscom/Icon SMI/Scott Bales, 19 (right)
Shutterstock/Pertusinas, tickets; Worldpics, soccer field

Essential content terms are **bold** and are defined at the bottom of the spread where they first appear.

Table of Contents

Best Save

Brazil and England clashed in the 1970 World Cup. Brazil's Pelé slammed a **header** to the open corner of the net. England's goalkeeper, Gordon Banks, leaped across the goal line. The ball looked like it would bounce over Banks. Pelé shouted, "Goal!" But Banks flicked the ball with one finger. He sent it high above the net. What a save!

header: a shot where players use their heads to hit the ball

5

Best World Cup Team

Brazil's 1970 World Cup team was not favored to win. Its star players all played **offense**. Most people thought **defense** won World Cup games. But Brazil's team of attackers started passing. Some goals included passes between seven or eight teammates. Brazil won every match and claimed the World Cup.

offense: when a team tries to score points

defense: when a team tries to stop points from being scored

Best Penalty Shot

The best **penalty shot** came in the 1999 Women's World Cup final. China made four of its five penalty shots. The United States scored on its first four shots. Then Brandi Chastain took the final penalty shot. The ball soared past the goalkeeper's hands and into the net. It gave the United States the win.

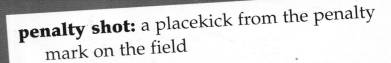

penalty shot: a placekick from the penalty mark on the field

Is It a Tie?

A 1986 World Cup quarterfinal came down to penalty shots. France's Bruno Bellone's shot powered into the goalpost and bounced straight out. The ball hit the Brazil goalkeeper's back and went into the goal. Was it better than Chastain's penalty shot?

Best Bicycle Kick

The best bicycle kick came in a 2006 match between Barcelona and Villarreal. Barcelona's Ronaldinho stopped a high crossing ball with a bounce off his chest. He flung his body around. He hooked the ball over his head with his foot. The ball sailed into the net.

Best Goal

In the 1986 World Cup, Diego Maradona scored the "Goal of the Century." Maradona got the ball near midfield. He dribbled untouched past five defenders. He dodged the goalkeeper and popped the ball into the net. Maradona's goal gave Argentina a 2-1 win over England.

Best Free Kicker

David Beckham's **free kicks** have a wicked spin. His skill has made curving banana kicks famous. He bends free kicks over a wall of defending players and into the goal. This talent started the expression, "Bend it like Beckham."

free kick: a placekick that is not on the penalty mark

Best Men's Player

Pelé is considered the world's best soccer player. He scored 1,281 goals in his 22-year career. He could play the ball out of the air and fire quick shots on goal. His eye for passing helped Brazil win three World Cup titles. In Brazil, Pelé is known as "The King."

Best Women's Player

In her 17-year career, Mia Hamm electrified the soccer field. She played in 275 international games for the United States. She scored a record 158 goals in those games. In 2001 and 2002, she was **FIFA's** player of the year. She also won two World Cups and two Olympic gold medals.

FIFA: the international governing body of soccer; FIFA stands for Fédération Internationale de Football Association.

Runner-up

Brazil's Marta is a rising soccer star. She is a fast forward with foot skills. Marta was FIFA's player of the year in 2008. She may earn the title world's best before her career is finished.

Best Goalkeeper

Russian goalkeeper Lev Yashin was known as the Black Spider. He wore a dark jersey. He could block amazing shots with a free arm or leg. Yashin held opponents scoreless in more than 200 games. He was voted the World's Best Goalkeeper six times. In 1971, Yashin retired after a 22-year career.

Italian Gianluigi "Gigi" Buffon is one of soccer's top goalkeepers. In the 2006 World Cup, he had five scoreless games. Opponents didn't score on him for 453 minutes in a row. Buffon earned the tournament's award for best goalkeeper.

Glossary

defense (di-FENS) — when a team tries to stop points from being scored

FIFA (FI-fuh) — the international governing body of soccer; FIFA stands for Fédération Internationale de Football Association.

free kick (FREE KIK) — a placekick that is not on the penalty mark

header (HED-ur) — a shot where players use their heads to hit the ball

offense (aw-FENSS) — when a team tries to score points

penalty shot (PEN-uhl-tee SHOT) — a placekick from the penalty mark on the field

Read More

Cline-Ransome, Lesa. *Young Pelé: Soccer's First Star.* New York: Schwartz & Wade Books, 2007.

Tieck, Sarah. *David Beckham.* Buddy Bios. Edina, Minn.: ABDO, 2009.

Whitfield, David. *World Cup.* Sporting Championships. New York: Weigl, 2008.

Internet Sites

FactHound offers a safe, fun way to find Internet sites related to this book. All of the sites on FactHound have been researched by our staff.

Here's all you do:

Visit *www.facthound.com*

FactHound will fetch the best sites for you!